W9-ATT-224

BESTIES FIND THEIR GROOVE

BY KAYLA MILLER & JEFFREY CANINO
ART BY KRISTINA LUU

CLARION BOOKS
IMPRINTS OF HARPERCOLLINSPUBLISHERS

Based on the Click series, created by Kayla Miller.

Clarion Books is an imprint of HarperCollins Publishers.
HarperAlley is an imprint of HarperCollins Publishers.

www.harperalley.com

Library of Congress Control Number: 2022934063
ISBN 978-0-35-852116-7 hardcover
ISBN 978-0-35-856192-7 paperback

Inks by Victor Martins
Color by Damali Beatty
Lettering by Lor Prescott
Illustrations, additional inks, and additional color by Kristina Luu
The artist used Clip Studio Paint with digital brushes to create the illustrations for this book.
Typography by Stephanie Hays
22 23 24 25 26 GPS 10 9 8 7 6 5 4 3 2 1

First Edition

For Mom, who helped me weather many formal wear–related crises —K.M.

For Katie and the Potato Sisters —J.C.

For Milo, my fluffiest best friend—rest in peace —K.L.

SNIFFLE
Noooooooooooo.
Strength, Beth.
We're almost to the best part.
But...why would Anil **do that** to Jaya?
She loved him, Chanda. She really loved him. She traveled back in time **twice** just to be with him.
Because he's a stupid, silly boy who doesn't know what's best for him.
Jaya deserves better, but the heart wants what the heart wants...
...or **whatever**.

They're **destined** to be together, though. That's what Jaya saw when she visited the future.
How can that happen if he says he can't be with a woman from the 22nd century?
Well, see, that was only one **possible** future. Anil could still totally mess up the happy timeline if he keeps being a fool.
But don't worry. He's going to come to his senses at his brother's wedding.
Speaking of: here we go!
- Where's Jaya, Anil? We thought she was your date for the wedding.
- She had to go back home. Wherever...*whenever*...that is.

ANIL!!
SNAP!
- Jaya?
- The future is nothing without you.

And Jaya and Anil lived happily ever after in the year 2189.
Z
Z
Z
That was the best movie I've ever seen. The singing! The dancing! The romance! The fashion!
Oh, Chanda, why isn't every movie like that?
Told ya Bollywood movies were good fun. **Samay Par**, particularly.
And to think I didn't start watching them until recently!
My mom had it in my head that the movies don't accurately represent life in India, that it's not all sprawling estates and big parties and blah blah blah...
I know she's right, but...
...there's no denying the outfits are incredible.

What a woman.

Okay, it's paused right before she snaps her fingers. I'm gonna hit play. Remember the steps?

I will **never** forget them!

HEY!

I've got an idea!

I should have known that permitting a school-night sleepover would result only in chaos and broken promises.

SMACK!!

POP!

MRRP

??

Whatever do you mean, Mother?

Beth and I had just finished our homework and were settling down for some **serious** sheep counting when Countess Pawsbury stepped on my laptop and made that music play. Silly Countess!

TUESDAY.
SNAP!
Can you put it up a little higher? It's looking uneven to me.
Unless I have a growth spurt in the next 10 seconds, this is as high as it's getting!

CHANDA!
Allow moi.
Thanks. I was starting to worry I'd become permanently stretched.
The giraffe over there sometimes forgets that we shorties down on the ground have our limits.
Hey, I asked if you wanted me to call Sawyer over here so you could stand on his head.
Join your friends for a Night of MUSIC, DANCING, and the ARTS at the
TRUE COLORS FUN-RAISER DANCE
Benefiting the Art and Theater Department of Bushmiller Middle School
FRIDAY MAY 20TH
DRESS TO EXPRESS!
TICKETS $5 PAYABLE AT DANCE!
SUPPORT YOUR SCHOOL!
A dance?!
With a *theme?!*
You bet! Trent and I had the idea to throw a fundraiser for the Art and Theater Department.
Their budget was cut pretty badly this year, and they might not be able to put on their spring show the way they want to without our help.

And Olive here had the idea for the **fun**-raiser to be a dance.
Fun. Fund. Get it?
The idea is that everyone comes dressed up all fancy in their favorite color, and at the door they put their admission fee into the jar that matches.
Fancy, eh?
Yeah! It's not like anyone has to wear a tie or anything—though that **is** a great tie, Chanda.
Merci.
I just thought it would be fun to dress up a little. This is our first school dance, after all.
It's a great idea, Liv. As I've said: I'll be there in my finest tie-dye.
Anyway, we should probably start dropping off these flyers at all the different homerooms.
See you dudettes later!

Our first school dance! And it's semifancy! What are you thinking: skirts at knees or ankles?
Think bigger, Beth. This is our chance to leave them all speechless.
Presenting Mademoiselles Chanda Basu and Elizabeth Wagner!
WOW!!
Who are they wearing?
Talented, brilliant, incredible, amazing, showstopping, spectacular, never the same...

Hold on—
where exactly are we finding outfits with that kind of magic power?

POP!

Beats me.

Well, we've got to take our doggy clients for a walk after school, but after that...

Closet deep dive?

It's a date.

I don't know, Beth. All of this stuff is cute, but most of it's just not special enough for the occasion.

Is there **nothing** that could work? Those are my best clothes.

I was thinking there would be at least **something** there we could pair with the runners-up from this pile.

Hey, there's a whole other half to that closet, isn't there?

Are you suggesting we look through darling sister **Lisa's** belongings?

What treasures have you been hiding from us, Lisa?

Okay, so where are all the dresses?
? ? ? ? ? ? ?

Twelve and a half years on this planet— have you ever seen me in a dress?

That...is not possible.
Come on, there's no way you wore slacks to a school dance.

Yeah, you're right. I didn't. I haven't **been** to any dances.
I've got more important things to worry about, like, oh, figuring out how I'm ever going to pay for college.

Knock, knock.
Ask, "Who's there?"

Who's there?
Baked ziti.
Baked ziti who?
Baked ziti's cookin', who's eatin'?

Not even a joke, Dad.
Maybe not, but you don't pay me for the jokes or the food. So, take what you can get.

Thanks for the offer, Mr. Wagner, but I've got to head home.
My sister is coming over to the house for dinner, and my mom insists that I be there.
Actually, she said it's okay if you come too, Beth.
Are you sure? I feel like it's been forever since you and Amaya had any sister-sister bonding time.
Exactly, which is why you absolutely **have** to come to dinner.
Looks like it's just you, me, and two heaping helpings of ziti, kiddo.
UH-HUH.

She's **here.**
Prepare for battle.
Hello, girls.
Need any help, Mrs. Basu?
Indeed. **Chanda,** would you please go upstairs and tell your didi that dinner is almost ready?
I'm afraid she probably has her head buried too deeply in her closet to hear me calling.
Of course Princess Amaya receives a special invitation to dinner instead of the typical holler.
Anything for the perfect daughter.
AMAYA!
DINNER!

Chanda?
Look at you! You look more mature and stylish every time I see you.
Beth! My goodness, it's been so long.
Thanks, Amaya. You too.
I don't know about more stylish, but I'm definitely getting **older**.
A piece of advice: Don't take your teen years for granted.
They'll be gone before you know it, and all you'll have left to remember them by will be about 50 boxes of stuff that your parents will absolutely insist you take with you when you move out.
NO WAY!
My sister's going off to college in the fall, which means I'll have our room to myself for the first time **ever**.
My parents will have to drag me out of the house if they want me to leave all that sweet new space behind.

Right—I'm sure your future sweetheart will love moving into your parents' house with you.
My *sweetheart?*
Okay, so where's my not-so-little sister hiding?
Uh, I guess she had to get something from her bedroom.
Your mom asked us to tell you that dinner's ready.
Oh, yum! I was promised all my favorites, so I think we're in for a feast.

We're happy you could find the time to join us, Chanda.
Chanda!

Amaya.

Your maa and I were just telling Amaya how proud of her we all are.
Graduating from school, landing all of her big job interviews, getting engaged to Seth... Right, Chanda?

SIIIIIP

Of course, we're sad to see our elder spreading her wings and flying from the nest, so to speak,
but we couldn't be more confident of the heights you'll soar to.

Proud.

My dad means well with his baked ziti, but I'd take your mom's dosa any day.
Actually, maybe I took too much.
Nothing. Not a stitch. Every dress I have that's even a tiny bit formal would make me look like a little kid playing dress-up.
Beth, our fashion sense has grown faster than our wardrobes.
You know, if Amaya is cleaning out her room, maybe she has some old dresses that might fit...
OKAY, BAD IDEA.
Hey, gals!
I'm sorry we didn't get a chance to chat more over dinner.
Mom and Dad have a tendency to carry on when they get all sentimental.

Whatcha up to?
Well, we're trying to pick out outfits for the school dance.
It's our first one, and we really want to make an impression.
A DANCE?!
Your first?!
Oh, gosh!!!
AAAAAAH!
Give me a second— I'll be right back!
Quick, let's barricade the door before—
I LOVE DANCES!
SCHOOL DAZE!
FWOOSH
What is that?
An old photo album! I came across it when packing earlier today.

Ha—look at me! What a little nerd I was.
I'm certain you girls will look a lot better than I did back then.
Tom
JUNIOR PROM
Liam
7th GRADE FORMAL
SENIOR PROM
Oliver
9TH GRADE HOMECOMING
I'm so excited for you. The first school dance is totally a rite of passage into your teen years.
I can't wait to see photos of you with your dates!
Brad
DATES?

Anyway, I've gotta get back to packing so I'm done by the time Seth arrives to help me cart it all away.
But keep my photo album for the time being. Maybe flipping through it will give you some ideas for your outfits.
Retro's in, right?

I'll be around the house all week, so let's gab more soon, okay?

CLICK!
. . .

DATES?!

I can't believe it took us this long to realize the obvious.

Of course we need dates. It's **essential** to the school dance experience.

Beth, we can't be the only kids who show up without them.

I don't know... I'm sure we'd still have a fun time without dates, and I don't think **everyone** is going to bring one.

Only a few of the people in our grade are officially "dating."

Every single person we know will have a date.

You don't need to be in a couple to have a date for a big dance. **Amaya** always had a date. So did all of her friends. You saw the pictures, Beth.

Nope. Wrong.
Dates for everybody, and I'll **prove** it to you.

How are you going to do that?
By asking the best sources of gossip we have—
—the cheerleaders!

Hey, Chanda! Wow, I **love** that look on you.
Beth! Classic, as always.

You're sweet to say so, Ava.
So, big dance next Friday. What's the word on the pavement? Who's pairing up?

You mean dates?
We're going with the football team.
Yeah—our coach insisted that it's "tradition."
Except that I found out this is the first sixth grade formal that's been held in, like, 10 years, so I don't know what she's on about.

It's sexist and outdated, is what it is. We're being treated like we're arm candy for the football players.

Worse, Coach wants us all to wear the school colors, but **of course** the boys got first choice, so we're stuck in yellow.

Bushmiller Middle School's cheerleaders are going to roll up to our first big dance looking like a bunch of bananas.

I'm not convinced.
First, the cheerleaders and football team are only two small groups of people.
Second, it seems like most of them **didn't want their dates** anyway. You're going to need more proof than that, Chanda.
Okey doke. If you insist...

Nick, Grace—you two going to the dance together?

. . .

Uh, we hadn't really talked about it!
What do you say, Nick?
Sure!

You **made** that happen, Chanda. That proves **nothing**!
Uh-huh, Beth. I'm sure you're right.

I think what we need to do is get back to the bigger issue at hand: **What** are we going to **wear?**

Hey, Hugh...

Got a date for the dance?

Yup. Asked Willow yesterday after school.
SECTION LEADER

All you've been doing is picking easy targets. **Of course** Hugh and Willow are going to the dance together.
A handful of people we know having dates for the dance doesn't mean that **everyone** will.
You're being dramatic, Chanda.
Oh, Beth. You fail to realize that I can be dramatic and still 100% correct.
Let's test my theory.
Hey, Olive. Need a hand?
YES PLEASE!!!
PUSH!
My heroes.
Do me a favor, though—**please** be here when I open it later.

So, before next Friday, I still have to make the colored jars, decorate Sawyer's costume, and get the playlist approved by Ms. Lin.
Say, Olive...

Going to the dance with anyone?

Huh? Oh, yeah.
I'm going with Trent and Sawyer.

...

Trent AND Sawyer?!

They **asked** you?

Well, Trent asked, but they're kind of a package deal.

Believe me yet?

Olive has **two** dates...
Exactly, which means if we're going to experience our first dance correctly and have the perfect night, we're going to need **at least** one date apiece.

If that's true, I hope they don't mind that we'll be wearing sweatpants.

Quit worrying! We can check off all the boxes in time.
Finding the perfect dresses is easy enough— we only need to figure out what we want and then beg your sister for a ride to the mall.
L-I-F-T

So, it's high time we start **visualizing** our dream ensembles...

WEDNESDAY NIGHT.

I think I can dazzle with something based on these...

I've been researching Desi fashion on the Internet and discovering one incredible look after another.

My mom wears some nice kurtas around the house, but those didn't prepare me for how fab these fits are.

If I can find anything close to these, I'll be in business.

What have you got on your mood board?

How's this?
-SPARKLES?
-RETRO??
-FITS!
-COMFORTABLY!
UNY

Well, uh, it's a place to start.

I know it's not much.
I guess I don't want to get any ideas that are too specific.
I can still remember the last time I went dress shopping...

It's okay. I'm sure something will jump out at you when we tear through the mall.
And with the money saved up from all the pet care we've been doing, we can shop the **front racks** at Eleganza for once. Bless those puppies and kitties.

Yeah, I'm sure you're right...

Okay, that's settled.
Onto securing our lucky suitors...

THURSDAY.
I've got a plan.
I've written down the name of every boy we know in the sixth grade, which is not as many as I would like, considering the situation.
If they're crossed out, that means they already have a date?
Precisely.
I expect that list to grow as I gather more intel, but at least we already know a few boys we shouldn't waste our time with.
HUGH
TRENT
SAWYER
NICK
FOOTBALL T
"Waste our time"? That's a crummy way to talk about our friends, Chanda.
You know what I mean.
Time is tight, and if we're going to make this work, we need to work quickly and scientifically.
If you say so...

B&C's BOY SAFARI

a study

DANCE!

SLIDE

NOD

NOD

ETHAN

·courteous

She should have gotten a dog rather than a cat.

Dogs shed too, but at least they're fun to play with.

BEN
·incompatible
MIKE
·BAD TASTE

!!

TURN

Whatcha reading?

A...book.

??

SLAM!

HMMMMMMMMM

DIEGO
·literate
·mysterious?

STEPHEN
IVAN
WURMZ!

??
WURMZ!

AHAH
HA
HA HA
HA

How'd the safari go?
SLAM!

Highly informative.

That's good.
Who are our dates?

Oh, Beth! Would that it were so simple!
I need to get home and do some serious calculations with all the data I've collected, but I should have something for us tomorrow morning if I pull an all nighter.

Actually, would you mind taking the dog-walking route by yourself today?
I guess I might need some time for homework, too.
No problem. Earning a little extra money for our shopping trip can't hurt.
Plus, it's only the sweet, big pooches today, so it'll be no sweat handling them alone.

Bye, Princess!
Bye, Milton!
Huh?!

B+C
PET PROFESSIONALS
What's up, Buddy? We've almost got you home!

I see how it is.
Someone isn't all played out yet?

All right then, **catch!**

You sweet, big, tireless fella.
B+C

B+C
RUB
RUB
Hey, Beth!

!!
B+C

I'm Sam!
I'd walk over to say hi, but it might take me a while.
SORRY!
Buddy wanted to play some more and I guess we got carried away.
Nah, I'm sorry for startling you. I guess it's kind of weird to hear a stranger call your name, huh?
Well, not a total stranger. We're in gym class together.
You're in Mrs. Griffin's homeroom, right? I'm in Mr. Moss's class. Old Mossy.
That's right! You're the Sam from gym class who—
—ate it pretty hard going for the impossible slam dunk. The one and only.
Got the broken leg to prove it.
Anyway, I just wanted to thank you for being so nice to Buddy.
Usually I'd be taking him for his walks after school, but I don't think I could keep up with him at the moment.

My parents hired the right person for the job.
Your T-shirt isn't lying—you really are a pet professional.

I don't know about that...
LICK!
B + C

I guess I should let you get going, huh?
Well, I'll see you in gym class. I'll be the one rooting you on from the bleachers.
Rooting me on?
Yeah! I've seen you play kickball—I wish I could kick half that well. Or, right now, **at all**.

G'night, Beth Wagner, Pet Professional!
B + C

FRIDAY MORNING.

BETH!

I've crunched the numbers!

Chanda... what numbers?

Is this about our math homework? Because, if so...

No! Our dates!

I've determined, scientifically, our best possible matches.

You have?

Beth, it's science.

Okay, so what has science decided for us?
That Ethan and Diego will be our dates to the dance.

Which one of us is going with which?
Unimportant.
I'll go with whichever one is taller.
??

But, Chanda, we hardly ever talk to Ethan or Diego...
Won't it be a little weird if we ask them to the dance out of nowhere?

Totally weird! Which is why **we're** not asking the boys.
They're going to ask **us**.

How are we convincing them to do that?
By turning on the charm, of course.

Good morning, Ethan.

Good morning, Diego.

FLUTTER

FLUTTER

RIIIIIIIIING
Goodbye, Ethan.
See you tomorrow, Diego.

SLAM

The seeds are germinating.

TWIRL
WHAT THE...?!
Lisa, guess what?!
It's Friday night!!
And we're feeling all right...
PLOP
But we'd all feel **a lot** better if you took us to the mall.

Believe me, I would if I could.
I'm in the middle of applying for these scholarships and...it's going to be a long night as it is.
It's like I've got to keep checking off all of these boxes before graduation, but the list keeps getting longer.
It's okay, Lisa.
Yeah—we're sorry you're feeling stressed.
How about I take you tomorrow after my shift at work?
YAY!
SIGH

SATURDAY AFTERNOON.

All right, squeaks, load out. I'll be back in two hours.

Huh?

You're...**not** coming with us?

Listen, I said I'd take you to the mall, but I've got errands to run.

Okay, maybe we don't **need** you to shop with us...
...but we really **want** you to. Can't you take a little break?

Yeah—we promise we'll try on some really awful dresses so you can have a good laugh.

A tempting offer, but I really don't have the time.

!!
KNOCK

!!

Claire. Becca. What's up?

Hey, Lis!
You here to pick up a new swimsuit for the beach trip?
You never responded to the group chat, but we're so happy you came!
All the gals can shop together now!
I can't. I'm just here dropping off my kid sister and her friend.
I'm really swamped with work this weekend.
It's a total pain.
That stinks.
You **are** coming on the trip, though, right? Annie wasn't sure...
Yeah, I'm hoping.
I've gotta finish some things before then. But...maybe?
Oh, okay. Well, we really hope you can make it.
Let us know if you need a ride. Claire and I are carpooling with Annie, and we'd love to have you along, teamie.
Absolutely. I'll text you.

Two hours.
I didn't know Lisa's lacrosse team was going on a trip.
Me neither. This is the first I'm hearing of it.
But she's been working so hard lately, it's not like she's been mentioning much to anyone.
GAME FAR
NEW
SALE
ELEGANZA
SALE
You know, I'm sorry for Lisa...
...but I'm grateful we have our priorities straight.

Can I help you with those?
No, thank you.
Miss, **please,** can I **help you** with those?!
Nope. Got it covered.
Find anything good?
Only one way to find out.

TAP
TAP

How's it going, Beth?
Awful.
KNOCK
That bad?
Worse.
Can I see?
Nuh-uh.
Beth.
MON DIEU!
That dress should be **illegal**.

Were the others that bad?
Ugh.
No...this is **definitely** the **worst**.

Some of the nicer dresses I picked out said they were my size, but they all fit too tightly in weird places.
And the ones that **do** fit make me look like I'm wearing a fancy garbage bag.

Do you want to try looking for a different size of the nicer ones?
I already took the biggest size they have...
Oh...

Did you find anything for you?

No.
They were all...**fine**. But nothing screamed **fantastic**.
And none of them looked much like the Desi clothes I'm feeling inspired by.

Shall we ditch this store and go poke around some others?
Uh, yes please.
DO NOT WANT
Oh, hey, Louisa!
Hey, Anna!
Beth! Chanda! Fancy meeting you here.
Hey, girls! Are you shopping for the dance too?

Yeeaaaaahhh.
Trying.
Nothing's clicking so far.

Imagine being in our boat—we're shopping for matching dresses!
Thankfully, we've got some definite contenders picked out to try on.

Will your **dates** be wearing matching colors too?
Oh, no, we don't have dates.

Oh. **Oh my.** I'm sorry for bringing it up.
We wish you luck with that, girls. There's still a week until the dance. We're sure you'll find dates in time.
??
?
???

Be grateful for our seeds, Elizabeth.

Anything?
Nuh-uh.
YOLO
SALE
Nope.
Yee Haw Supplies
Wanna just go smell fancy soaps until Lisa comes to pick us up?
Definitely.
BATH

Find what you were looking for?
We didn't come in search of disappointment, but that's all we found.
Chanda, what are we going to do?
I suppose we could try searching online for dresses that would arrive in time.
But even if they did, there's no guarantee they'd fit...
I don't know...
Maybe we need to look through our closets again.
Unless...

Hey, Lisa, wanna drive us into **the city** to go shopping?
I heard about some colleges there you might want to tour.
Tour some colleges on a Saturday night in the city that's two hours away, that costs $30 in tolls to drive into, and that Mom would destroy me if I ever let you two roam around in unsupervised?
Sure, let's go.
Closets it is.
Have either of you considered, y'know, **not** dressing up for the dance?
. . .
Yeah, sorry, just trying to contribute. I've got nothing.

Give me...your **threes**.
Why, I **do** believe you must go fishing.
I will do no such thing.

?!
That's the **point** of the game. If you guess wrong, you have to go fish.
Well, I don't see what's so fun about that, and I'm not playing.
SMACK!
Chanda, it's Saturday night.
I'd rather not keep feeling grumpy until we pass out from exhaustion.
How can you joke at a time like this?
Because what else am I supposed to do?! We don't have dresses, we don't have dates...
You know what? I say we throw in the towel and just pretend we're sick next week and can't go.
Easy! Done.

WHAT!
HUFF
Lisa, tell me...
Uh-huh?
Applying for scholarships and working a part-time job all while trying to graduate from high school.
Sounds pretty tough.
Feel like giving up?

Nope.
Good, Lisa. Smart, Lisa.
Be like **Lisa**, Beth.

Listen, I don't **not** want to go to the dance. I just...
I'm having a hard time figuring out why it has to be this stressful.
Perfection isn't easy, Beth. And it isn't always **fun**, either.
Then **why** are we trying to be perfect??
Because...it matters.
To who??
To **everyone**.
Lisa, you're pretty much perfect. Tell us: Does being perfect matter?
Sure—it matters to college admissions committees.
I **don't** think we'll be applying to college with personal essays about how perfect our first middle-school dance was.

That's not the point. Perfection...is a state of mind.
One perfect evening that checks off all the boxes could set us on the right path for life.
I know it might not seem like it matters, like it's just a silly dance, but people **are** watching.
Our friends, our teachers, our siblings—
I'm not watching.
Our **parents**.
They're watching and they're judging.
It's either "Oh, Beth and Chanda—they sure are going places in life!"
Or "Ugh—**Beth** and **Chanda**."
It's your choice, Beth. Pick!
I'm not saying we shouldn't care about stuff or try to impress people sometimes. Isn't that why we own and operate the most successful preteen pet-care business in the tri-county area?
But I think we can have fun at the school dance without making it feel like work, too.

Even perfect Lisa knows how to put the work away and have fun sometimes.
Isn't that right?

Yeah. Sure. Fun. Getting right on that.

C'mon, you know what I mean. You're working hard **now** so that you can go on that beach trip with your team, yeah?

Wrong.
I'm not going on any beach trip.

What? Why not? You love the beach.

Because...
...I have more important stuff to worry about than eating funnel cake on the boardwalk and catching rays.

Even if I get all of these applications submitted on time, I still have a huge backlog of projects from school I should be working on.

So, no, I don't think the sun and I will be seeing much of each other for a while...
And frankly, I really can't understand how you two can afford to spend so much time worrying about dances and dresses and dates, anyway...
TURN
Don't they assign homework in middle school anymore?
Lisa's right, Beth.
I hate to admit it, but we'll probably need to start doing better in math class if perfection is our ultimate goal.
So...we're spending **Saturday night** doing homework now?

Polly wanna whatever-these-are?

Her name is **Tabitha,** and Mrs. Foyle says she sleeps much better if you use her name when addressing her.

Okay.

Tabitha wanna these-things?

Baxter has been waiting at the door since he finished his breakfast.
I dare say he adores his Sundays at the park with his favorite girls.

A wonderful morning...
No planning or stress required!
B+C PET
B+C PET

Bye, Princess!

See you soon, Milton!

We'll miss you too, Baxter.

Hi, Sam!
??

??
"Hi, Sam"?

Hi, Beth.
Hi, Chanda.
I'm—

HMPHHH

dooFF
Little help?

I think I misjudged this hangout spot.

I'm Sam.

Sam, eh?
??
Yeah—we have gym together.

FWIP!
??
SAM
-temporarily out of commission
-clearly clumsy on feet
↳probably a bad dancer?
NOD
Of course.
Impossible-Slam-Dunk Sam.
HA HA
Not my proudest moment...
But it's done wonders for my name recognition around school.
So Buddy is your dog, huh? He's a real sweetie.
Isn't that right, **Beth?**

Huh?
Sweet??
Yes! Right—**Buddy** is the sweetest.
??

Say, Beth, I was wondering...

Yes, Sam?
B + C

Um, well—I was, uh, wondering...

• • •

Was Buddy a **good boy** today?

Yes, he's the sweetest. We've established that.
That's what you wanted to ask us?
Uh...yes?
OooooKAY, THEN.
You and Buddy have a great day, now. Remember to help Sam with his homework, Buddy!
Seems like he might need it...

Do you want to come over for dinner tonight?
Amaya is going to be there again, and this time with the wondrous Seth, fiancé and future beloved son-in-law.
I can't, sorry.
My mom has the night off work, and I promised her we'd make dinner together. The world-famous quiche.
If we can rope Lisa into helping, it'll be a real Wagner women bonding experience.
Of course, you're welcome to join us.
But it sounds like you'd probably be missed at your house.
Yeah...There's no way out of this one.

...AMAYA...

...OF COURSE!...

...SWEET SETH...

...PERFECT PRINCESS...

..."OH, CHANDA!"...

CHANDA! BEAUTIFUL TIMING.

I'd say the sibling psychic connection is still strong between us.

AMAYA.
How's my favorite little sister doing?
Fine. I'm fine.
Just out here minding my own business.
It feels like I haven't seen you in forever, Chanda.
Same.
Mom and Dad say Chanda is so busy with her pet-care enterprise that some days they only see her as a blur zooming out of the house toward her next furry client.
Wow, impressive!
Business is that booming, huh?

Uh-huh.
You could say we're in demand.
ZOOM
Learn anything interesting about the neighborhood pets?
Sure.
Mrs. Foyle's parrot will eat anything **but** crackers.
Hold up a second, Chanda.
Let's do some strategizing.
Okay, so if Mom and Dad start carrying on about Seth and me and the wedding again, let's try to swerve the conversation to a different topic.
I'm certain both of us could use a break from the Amaya Celebration Hour.
Sure...

Our code words will be “Mrs. Foyle’s parrot.”

AMAYA!!

Amaya
Amaya
Amaya.
Amaya.
Amaya Amaya
wedding plans
Amaya. Amaya?
Amaya!
House hunting
Amaya
Amaya
Amaya.
Amaya
Amaya—
Seth!
B+C
PET
Seth Seth Seth, Seth—
a good head on his shoul
Seth Seth Seth.
Hey, Chanda. What was that you were telling me about **Mrs. Foyle's parrot?**
LEAN
Thanks for dinner, Mom...Dad.
Please excuse me. I don't feel well, and I have a lot of homework left to finish before bed.
SKREE

Hey, Chanda. You left me hanging at dinner.
Is anything the matter?
Sorry.
I'm not feeling very well all of a sudden.
Well, Seth and I are heading out soon, so I wanted to wish you good night...
Good night.

Good night, sis.
CLICK
MRRROW?
Yeah, Countess, I know...

SIGH.
What makes Amaya so evil is that she's the **perfect** sister, too.

I wish she and her perfectly perfect fiancé would hurry up with their perfectly perfect wedding and find their perfectly perfect house so we could all forget about them and their perfectly perfect life.
PURRRRR

Wouldn't that be **perfect?**

MONDAY.

So, I'm thinking we spend today nurturing our seedlings.

For example, we can let Ethan and Diego hold the door open for us as we leave homeroom.

Holding the door open requires... both of them?

Beth, we can't nurture only one seedling and leave one shriveled and neglected.
It's already **Monday**. We need two strong, flowering plant boys by Wednesday, at the **absolute latest**.
Hey, if all we need is a couple of plants to bring us to the dance, my mom has some philodendrons we could pair with just about any outfit.

Gee, thanks, Beth. Great contribution. Happy to know we're both taking this so seriously!
HAHAHAHA!
HEY, BETH!

Hold on...

Just a second...

There. Sorry about that.
Beth, I was wondering if I could talk to you for a minute?

Alone, that is...

Oh! Sure. Yeah—
—of course!
Meet you inside, Chanda?
Suuuure...
I wanted to talk to Ava real quick anyway.
Considering she's stuck dressing up like a banana for the dance, I figure she might let me raid her closet this week.
So what's up, Sam?
Ha-ha.
So, this...might sound silly...
...and I know I probably wouldn't make for the best dance partner...

...but I was wondering...

...Beth Wagner...

...WOULD YOU MAYBE WANT TO...

...and the parrot snatched the lip balm right out of my hand!
HAHA!
I had to keep telling her she didn't have lips to use it on before she was finally convinced to drop it.

Chanda, your stories are the perfect way to start my day.

And you're **more than welcome** to stop by my place anytime to dig through my closet.
Though I suspect nothing I own would do you justice.
Thanks, Ava.

Maybe all I'll need to dazzle everyone at the dance is to wear Tabitha as a fascinator.
Chanda...
Something... happened.
So...you know Sam, right?
Slam-Dunk Sam. Boy we talked to yesterday. Boy you were just having a secret meeting with.
Hmm, doesn't ring a bell.
He...asked me to the **dance**.

AND I...
...SAID YES.
Chanda, are you okay?!
SLAM
STAGGER
But...
...our seedlings.
I'm sorry, Chanda. I know this wasn't part of your plan.
But...I didn't want to say no.
It's fine. I'll just...
I'll need to accelerate things.
HUFF

WHOOSH!
Good morning, Ethan.
Did you have anything you wanted to ask me??
SLAM!!
I—I don't think I do?

Diego...
WHIRL!
...do you have anything you'd like to—

No.

Chanda...

...are you okay?

I'm perfectly fine.

12
9
3
6
RIIING!
Do you want to talk about it?
What's there to talk about?

Clearly, I need a more direct approach.

Oh no—Sam!
I've gotta go help him, Chanda.
!!

My party is on its last leg, our cleric fallen, the monstrous Gorvil one hit away from our obliteration...
...and **that's** when I roll a natural 20 and—
SLAM!
Tyler Dewberry...
Have **I** got an offer for **you**.
??
Gonna need Tyler alone for a moment, Sawyer.

This is my locker.
Go eat lunch.
Hey, you don't have to tell me twice to eat lunch.
SLAM!
Later, Tyler.
Uh...
Can I go eat lunch too?

Not quite yet.
We have an important matter of business to discuss first.
Here's what I'm proposing...
The school dance is this Friday.
Big deal. **Everyone's** going to be there.
But, importantly, if you're going to do it right, it's essential to have a date.
Thus, it would be good for the both of us if we went to the dance together.
As **dates**.
So, Tyler Dewberry...
Will you go to the dance with me?
No.

Excellent. You'll pick me up Friday at—
WAIT.
WHAT!
No, I will **not** be your date for the dance.
But—but why not?! This is a win-win. You win, I win...
Our **proud friends and family** win.
Tyler, it's a win-win-**win**.
I'm saying no because I'm surprised you even remember my name.
We hardly know each other, and you've never talked to me outside of class before.
Also, I'm feeling confident from your presentation that this isn't a secret-hidden-crush situation.

Are you only asking me because nobody asked **you?** Because you assumed I wouldn't already have a date and would automatically say yes?
Well, when you put it like that...
I'd rather go to the dance alone than go with someone who is asking me as their last resort.
To be fair, you weren't the **last** resort.

Just forget it.
Tyler, wait.
We can still work this out to benefit the both of us.
I'm sorry you don't have a date for the dance, Chanda.
But you're not the only person in the world with feelings.
I know that...

Chanda, are you okay? We were getting worried.
I couldn't find you anywhere after I helped Sam with his books.
FOOD!

Yeah, sorry. I had something I thought I had to do.
Turns out, not so much...

Wanna talk about it?
Maybe later.

WHAT'S A GIRL...

...HAVE TO DO...

...TO GET A DATE!!

B+C
PET
PROFESSIONALS

I don't understand...
You got a date without even **trying** while I was rejected by **three different people** today!!
What did you do to get Sam to ask you?
Gee, I didn't really do anything.
I guess I was just being myself and—

THAT DOESN'T MAKE SENSE, BETH!
...

HUFF
I'm sorry for blowing up.
I'm obviously frustrated, and I know I can be a pain to be around when I get like this.
PHEW.
I guess I haven't cracked the boy code yet.
I'm Jaya before the wedding, looking for the right dance moves.
But, then again, a date's a date, right?
Maybe I should take Tabitha to the dance as my escort rather than my accessory.

See you tomorrow...

Good night.

Beth! You're home!
Get in here! Dad brought us a surprise.

DOUGHNUTS!
Dad said we could each have one before dinner...

...and I saved you your favorite!

NO.
No thanks, Johnny.

FWOOP!!

HEY.

RUSTLE

AAP
Hey, Lisa...

grumble
Can I talk to you about something?

Sure.

Gotta make it quick, though.

I have to go to the library to scan in this application before my shift at the grocery store. And then I've also somehow got to find time to study for the AP bio exam...

...which maybe I can do during my shift if the cool manager is on and it's a slow night, but there's no guarantee of that, so I'm probably going to have to study in my car for the hour beforehand.

We can talk later, Beth.
You know you can always talk to me about anything.
Yeah...
...except when I can't.

MEANWHILE...
!?
No way...
Two nights in a row?!
Is she trying to torture me??
Looks like Mrs. Foyle's parrot and I are study buddies tonight...
CHANDA—HEY!

SWIVEL
I've been keeping a lookout for you, sis!
Seth and I gave Mom and Dad a gift certificate to the new Italian restaurant downtown so they could have a date night—
—and so that you and I could have a sister-date night!
JOY.
You know I'm **12,** right?
I **don't** need a babysitter.
I know that! I'm not here to keep an eye on you...
I'm here to spend some quality time with the coolest little sister a girl could ever ask for!

I also thought we could make dinner together!
I've been itching to have you and the 'rents try this amazing sweet noodle casserole Seth's grandmother taught me how to cook.
EGG NOODLES
COTTAGE CHEESE
SOUR CREAM

Do we **have** to make dinner together?
I'd be fine eating some cookies and calling it a night.

No way!
Seriously, Grandma Geller's kugel is like eating dessert for dinner. You're gonna love it.

Fill me up a pot of water to boil, will ya?

FSHHH

Okay, so why don't you mix those together while I mind the noodles and find that casserole dish I know is here somewhere...
There you are!
SPLOOSH
You'd think a **biochemist** would be a little more observant...
SHAAAA

So...what do you think?
Tell Seth's grandma: "Pretty good."
Tell her yourself! You'll be seeing her at the wedding this summer.
Ah, yes, **the wedding.**
Speaking of the wedding...
I was showing Seth all of the photos you've been taking and posting online, and he loves them as much as I do.
We were wondering if you'd come scout out the venue with us. Help us figure out all the optimal places for everything.
We think you have **such** a good eye for those sorts of things.
What—
are you trying to get me to take photos at the wedding for free or something?
NO!

. . .

What is with this attitude you've been taking toward me lately?!

Chanda, if something is bothering you, you can always talk to me about it.

After all, we're sisters...

YOU WOULDN'T UNDERSTAND!
CHANDA,
WAIT!
STOMP!
STOMP!
SLAM!
PLOOMF!

KNOCK KNOCK
Quite the way to thank me for dinner.
BOOF!!
Come on, sis. Tell me what's going on.
You wouldn't understand...
How could you understand? You're perfect. You're good at everything and things always go exactly the way you want.

And then there's **me**...
...a grade-A mess.
SHAKE
PRR
That is patently **untrue**.
We're just good at different things.
You're creative and artistic and fashionable...
...and **I** have **no idea** what looks good and what doesn't.
The last time I went shopping, I bought three versions of the same skirt in different shades of gray.
Felt like the **practical** thing to do.
And now I'm supposed to pick out flowers and tablecloths and bridesmaid dresses and a million other things for this wedding of mine...
PRRRR

I could **really** use a super stylish little sister to help me figure it all out.
Gee, it must be hard for you to have the first difficult situation of your life at age 24...
I can't even finish the sixth grade without making a total joke of myself!
Ever since you told me I needed a date for the dance, I have been trying to find one...
...and have been rejected by three boys. **THREE**.
Add on that I'm pretty sure I hurt my best friend's feelings in the process...
So, yeah. Anyone waiting for me to become the perfect daughter or sister or friend is going to be waiting forever.
B+C

Okay, first off, no one—
—not me, not Mom, not Dad, not Beth, not your friends, not your teachers, **no one**—
—expects you to be perfect.
So get that right out of your head.
Second, I never told you that you needed a date for the dance.
Where'd you get that idea?
You always had one.
In every single dance photo, you have some guy on your arm and look like America's sweetheart.
You've still got my photo album, right?
Where is it?
Notice anything?
Yeah, that you lived the perfect teenage life.
No. Look closer—
It's true I always had a date, but it's also **always** a different boy.

I remember feeling like you did, that I simply **had** to have a date, but all that resulted in was me looking at these boys like they were accessories rather than people.

I haven't spoken to any of them in years...

But do you see who the constant is in all these photos?

My friend Libby. You remember her, right?

Gosh, we used to have so much fun together. In fact, I know I would have had a lot more fun at all these dances if I'd gone with Libby and my other girlfriends instead of worrying about our silly dates.

She and I never drifted apart, either.

At the wedding, she's going to be one of my bridesmaids alongside you.

Wanna know how Libby and I first met?

In the seventh grade, we both **lost** in the second round of the spelling bee.

But that meant we got to sit next to each other for the whole rest of the tournament, misspelling each new word that came up to make each other laugh.

And you know how I met the love of my life?

By chance in the library during finals week, when we both weren't looking where we were going and walked directly into each other.

You can't **plan** for everything to turn out perfectly, Chanda.

All you can do is leave yourself open for the possibility of perfection falling into your lap.

SIGH.

I've got a lot of apologizing to do.

TUESDAY.
You've got this.

Maybe everyone will simply **sense** that I'm sorry and I won't need to say anything.

Fiiiiiiiiine.
be POSITIVE!
SIGH.

Ethan...
I'm sorry for putting you on the spot like that yesterday. It was uncalled-for.
?!

Umm...okay...
Apology... accepted?

NOD

Diego, I'm sorry for—
It's whatever.
SPACE KID

You will always be a mystery to me, Diego.
I thank you for this.

Hi, Beth.
Hey...
You got my text, right?
Yeah. Amaya drove you to school, huh? Must have been **fun**.
It was...all right.
We had a good talk last night, actually.
Really?
You and...Amaya... **talked?**
Yeah, I know. I'm surprised too.
Anyway, it helped me realize I've been looking at things the wrong way.
I don't need a date to have fun at the dance. If it's not to be, it's not to be.
But I'm also **really happy** that you found one. I'm sorry if yesterday it sounded like I wasn't.

What have you and Sam got planned, anyway?
Are you going to give him a boutonniere?
I need **details,** Elizabeth.
Are his parents going to pick you up?
Is he going to give you a corsage?
We...haven't talked about it.
I don't know...
I might tell him I can't go to the dance with him after all.
I still don't have anything to wear, so what's the point?
Maybe I should just stay home.
WHAT?!

Beth, no.
You **have** to go.
I can't imagine the dance without you.
And we still have time to find the right dresses, if that's what's worrying you.
I'm not sure how, but we'll figure it out.
As a first step, you're welcome to anything you find in my closet.
My dresses might be old news to me, but they'd probably look stunning on you.
I don't think anything of yours would fit me...
RIIIIIIIING

AFTER SCHOOL...
All right then...
Let's see what we have to work with.

Chanda—
!!
—what is going on here?

Nothing **successful.**
Beth and I still don't have dresses to wear to the dance on Friday.
We couldn't find anything at the mall last weekend, and I've been through my closet **twice** trying to find something even close to what either of us imagined...
PURRRRR
No luck.

We made these mood boards for inspiration.
But I guess our dream styles aren't what's trending.
You've put a lehenga choli on yours.
That's what Jaya wears in **Samay Par**.
I can't stop thinking about her outfit. Desi clothing is so beautiful, and I feel like my wardrobe has been missing out on it all my life.
But are you sure you'd want to wear something like this to your dance?
It would look very different from what the other kids will be wearing.
I'm done worrying about what other people think.
What really matters is how I feel.
I want to wear what feels right for me.

Follow me.
I might have something that could help.
See if this is anything like what you've been dreaming of.
Oh, Mom.
It's **gorgeous**.

This was something I brought with me when I moved to the United States long ago, when I was your age.

I always loved its color and patterning, but outside of some family weddings, I didn't have many opportunities to wear it.

Everyone I knew, even all the Desi kids, dressed like the teenagers they saw in American movies and TV shows, so it would never have crossed my mind to wear something like this to a school dance.

It's perfect.
Thank you so much, maa.
I know your father and I have been focused on Amaya lately. With all the big changes going on in her life, it's difficult not to be.
But don't let that lead you to believe we don't see the impressive young woman you're becoming.
Thank you, beti, for always having the confidence to be yourself.

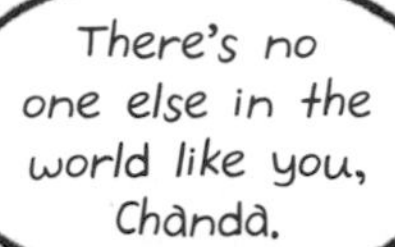
There's no one else in the world like you, Chanda.
Papa, Amaya, and I are fortunate to call you ours.

However, you **will** need to find a different top if you want to wear the lehenga to school.
Naturally.

SIGH

??
What's wrong?

My problem is solved, but that doesn't help Beth out of hers.

Wait a minute...
Can I borrow your cell phone?

WEDNESDAY.

Good morning, sweetheart.
Mornin', Mom.
Interesting getup.
Is it telling me you're due for a laundry day?
No...
Well, probably, but...
I'm just not feeling very stylish today.
Okay, **now** I'm concerned.
Are you coming down with something?
No, Mom. I'm fine, but I'm running late.
I'll see you tonight...

G'morning.
Hey.
So, that science homework last night, right?
Mr. Moss doesn't need to work that hard to prove to me I don't know much about rocks.
Yeah.
That one took a while...

Hey, Beth!
Beth...
I just don't know what to tell him yet.
Before you tell him anything, let's take one last look through your clothes after school.
Please?

I don't see how that's going to help. We've been through my stuff already.
Unless you can cast a magic spell and turn me back into a cute eight-year-old who fits into my old dresses, I'm out of options.
You've gotta trust me, is all.
If anyone can find their way out of a fashion nightmare, it's us.
Okay, this might sound a little weird, but bear with me...

Put this on.
No—around your eyes!
What are you up to, Chanda?
I'm not really in the mood for games, if you haven't noticed.
What did I say about trusting me?
We're never going to make it out of middle school if you don't start having a little faith!
CREEAK!
RUSTLE RUSTLE
SQUEAK!
THUD
Uh, can I look now?
SLIP ZIP
ZIP! ZOOM!
SLAM
Shaaa
NOT YET!
ZIP
Slip
SRRRRRREEE
EEE
ZIP!
SHAK

Okay...
Now.
TA-DA!

Welcome to your own personal secondhand boutique, ma chérie.
Chanda... your outfit...
Where did you...?
It's my mom's, from when she was our age.
When I told her about the trouble we were having, she pulled this out of her closet.
And it got me thinking...
Maybe **your** mom has something hidden away for **you** to wear too.
And she was right.
I went to my fair share of formal events as a youngster, and I could never bear to get rid of any of the dresses.
They might not be exactly what you were hoping for, but I'd like to think your old ma was pretty stylish back in the day.

Do you see anything you like?
They're all... so **beautiful**, Mom.
But this is the dress.
I wore that one to my senior ball.
Try it on, sweetheart.

I was a little bit taller and wider than you as a teen, but with some alterations we can get this to fit you just right.
Come to think of it, I'm certain this dress came with a matching wrap.
I'll check my closet and see if I can unearth it.
Done.
Go take a look.

You look fabulous, Beth.

What's the matter?
We've done it! We found you the perfect dress.
I know...
...and I'm so grateful.
It's just that...I've been feeling so bad about how I look ever since we went dress shopping at the mall.
None of the pretty dresses we found were made for someone with a body like mine.
I guess I was starting to feel like maybe I didn't **deserve** a pretty dress.
And when you were so surprised that Sam had asked me to the dance...
...I felt like maybe I didn't deserve a **date**, either.

I'm so sorry I made you feel that way, Beth.

Me being surprised about you and Sam had nothing to do with you and everything to do with me being afraid I was doing something wrong.
Which I **totally was,** though I guess in more ways than I thought.

Of course you deserve a date.
You deserve everything.
You deserve to have an amazing night at the dance and to feel good about yourself.
And most of all you deserve to see yourself the way that **I** see you.
The way that everyone we know sees you...

As the strong, kind, and beautiful Beth we love.

Thank you, Chanda. That means a lot to hear.

When I looked in the mirror just now...
...that's exactly how I felt—
—BEAUTIFUL.

But sometimes it's hard to remember that feeling when everything around me seems to be telling me I'm not.
I don't see girls like me popping up on TV or in movies or magazines very often.

I think I understand the feeling.
When I look at those same things, I don't see many Indian girls.

I guess that's why I felt like I had to find an outfit like Jaya's in the movie.
She's so cool and confident and bold and stylish.
And she looks like **me**.

Y'know...
...if the world isn't going to give us a lot of style icons to look up to, maybe we'll have to be our own.
I could live with that.
Well, I couldn't find the wrap, but that's no big loss.
Look at you two! You'll be the belles of the ball.
I'll be around tomorrow to help you make any alterations you need.
You don't mind if your old dress gets cut up?
Trust me— the next "senior ball" I attend will have a very different dress code.

THURSDAY.
Mornin', Sam.
Need any help carrying those books to class?

That would be great, thanks.
I keep asking for them to install bookshelves on these crutches of mine...

We're happy to help in the meantime.

Hey, Beth, so...
...I wanted to talk to you about our plans for tomorrow night.

My sister offered to drop all three of us off at the dance.
Want us to pick you up at seven?

Yeah, that would be great.

Second question:
What color dress are you wearing?

RAPPARAPPA RAPPA

This is like witnessing fashion magic.

ARAPPA BRRR RAPPA RAPPA BRRR

Hey.

What's going on?

The library. Studying.
Not that it's any of your business.
Poor Lisa Wagner.
She spent so much time at the library that the librarians shelved her with the reference books on accident.
She was never seen again.
What, no comeback?
The situation is worse than we thought.
You win this round, squeak.
But only because I'm operating on about five hours of sleep.
Well, Lisa, if you need a little fun and relaxation...
...I'm about done altering this dress, and we've still got **a lot** of Mom's old ones left over.
??
Wanna let us dress you up and give you a makeover?

NOPE.
ZOOM
Johnny makeover?
Johnny makeover.
I'll pretend I didn't hear that.
HA
HA
HA
CHIPS

FRIDAY.
THE DAY OF THE DANCE.

Streamers?
Check.
Balloons?
Check.
Twinkle lights?
Hmm...
Did we **forget** the **twinkle lights?!**
No, no—check.
I just always called them "sprinkle lights"... 'cause they're all different colors, like sprinkles?
Learn something new every day.

So, I think our new plan for a perfect evening is much more manageable.
It was pretty brutal before.
I see that now...
The new plan has an **entirely different** philosophy. It's only three steps long!
Okay, I trust you. Lay it on me.
Step 1?
Head to my house after school and change into our outfits.
Easy.
Step 2?
Wait for Lisa to pick us up. Maybe take some pics if my parents insist, which they probably will.
Pick up Sam on the way.
Long step, but okay.
Step 3?
Arrive at our final destination:
Fun City.

Is it time?
6:00 on the dot.
Prepare for action.

We're ready!

Oh, girls, you look...
...amazing!
...pretty good.

I put it on autofocus...
Papa, just press the big red button.

You know...
...I don't think we should pass up the rare opportunity to capture all of these lovely sisters gathered together.

Ready to hit the road?

Nope!

Sorry— forgot my clutch upstairs. BRB!

After you, milady...

When Chanda gets back, make sure to tell her I did this for you.

I **need** to see the envy on her face.

Hey, now that you've got me all to yourself...

What was it you wanted to talk to me about the other night?

Being bigger than most girls my age has never bothered me before.

But lately I've been feeling like everything's been telling me that it **should**.

And even if I like how I look tonight, I'm worried about how I'll feel the **next** time I run into something that tells me I'm wrong for being the size I am.
Am I supposed to want to change?
The only thing that needs to change is a society that would convince the world's cutest 12-year-old to feel bad about herself for even a second.
I know that it can be hard to ignore the negative feedback out there.
And that sometimes even the good feedback—like a boy who normally only sees you in sweaty gym clothes asking you to the dance—doesn't make you feel any better.
But if you love yourself, you're off to a good start.
Thanks, Lisa.
Hey, I'm always good for a pep talk.
And you love me too, right?
Oodles of love, squeak.

So where does this Sam live, anyway?
Not far. We'll direct you.
And what about you, Chanda?
Do we have to make a pit stop for any date you managed to wrangle for yourself?

It's hard to believe, **I know**, but I don't have a date.
And that's perfectly okay.

Exactly. I mean, I'm happy I'm going with Sam and all...
...but I'm mostly excited to be spending my first dance ever with all my friends.

Evenin', ladies!

It's kind of you to escort me to our chariot.

WORM ART

Before we go...
Sorry I can't tie it on for you.
That's okay. I **love** tying things.
And wait a second...
I think I felt something else down here.
I didn't know what color your outfit would be...
...but what **doesn't** go with cream?
I believe you did it, Samuel.
You finally landed an impossible slam dunk.

Have a fun night, kid.

You too!

SHOW YOUR TRUE COLORS
FUN RAISER

AHEM.
Attention, everyone.
TAP
TAP
We'll be starting the night momentarily with "a slowy but a goody."
So if you're looking for that magical moment with a special someone, I'd suggest hitting the dance floor now.
So, um, Beth...
Wanna dance?
Yes, please.

May I have this dance?
Are you only asking because you assumed I'd automatically say yes?
I've been wanting to apologize for how I treated you the other day.
HAH!

It was rude and insensitive and totally fueled by my misplaced priorities.
You didn't deserve it.
Thanks.
Apology accepted.
I'm glad you said no, by the way.
Even if it felt bad at the time, it put me in the timeline I needed to be in to get to where I am.
Might sound weird, but I felt just like the robot-building, time-traveling hero in this movie I love.
She had to be rejected before she could—
Jaya of the 22nd century?
Samay Par?

?!
You watch Bollywood movies too?
Sure. I'll watch anything science fiction.
Samay Par is a science-fiction romance.
I'm not opposed to, um, a little romance in movies...
...as long as the science is, uh, grounded in real principles and theories, of course.
Hey, Chanda...
?!
Want to dance together?
OH?

Yeah, my "date" thinks he's too cool to dance and just wants to stand around in the corner with his friends instead.
Plus, just between us...
...I'd much rather be dancing with you.
WELL...
I'd sort of already promised this dance...
No, please. Feel free.
PHEW!
I was mostly bluffing with the offer anyway.
You sure?
Positive.
Crowds... Slow dancing... Not really my strengths.
Thanks, Tyler Dewberry.
I'm glad we had this chat.

You look great, by the way.
Not at all banana-ish.
Thanks!
And you look...
WOW.
But I wouldn't expect anything else from you.
Why so quiet?
Is something wrong?
?
No...

...I'm just enjoying a perfect moment.

Now that we've got the obligatory slow song out of the way...
IT'S PARTY TIME!

FUN
RAI
SER

BRIDAL
FLORAL
You're INVITED

SNAP!

A Q&A WITH THE BESTIES TEAM

Q: What was different about working with your collaborators on book two versus book one?

KAYLA: Not to be too cute about it, but I think we "found our groove." Seeing the first book finished helped us picture what the finished art in this book would look like and allowed us to write scenes where we knew Kristina's art would shine.

JEFFREY: I must agree with Kayla. The biggest difference for me was having learned all of Kristina's strengths as an artist over the course of working on ***Besties: Work It Out***. The script for book one was written with only a few samples of Kristina's art for the series in hand, so I largely pictured a version of Kayla's style in my mind when writing that script. But, after seeing all that Kristina brought to the table in book one, I felt confident going for more emotion, drama, and dynamic visual storytelling when writing ***Find Their Groove***. There's nothing Kristina can't draw to perfection.

KRISTINA: By now, I think we all had a pretty good idea of what everyone's strengths were, and we just had to modify them to work even better together and to really shine. That's the best kind of collaborative work—when something is greater than the sum of its parts. This book was even more collaborative than the first. We also expanded the art team to include Victor, our inker. With three people on the art team, it really felt like a full-team effort, and I couldn't be more proud of what we accomplished. With Kayla and Jeffrey's whip-smart and heartfelt writing, Victor's beautiful background work, and Damali's lovely colors, I think we've made something really special. This book speaks to me on so many levels, and I think the love and care everyone's poured into it really shows.

DAMALI: Working on this book was different, but I can't really complain, because I feel like our workflow as a team got a lot smoother. Working on the first book was a bit tough, but coming back for book two was a bit like saying hi to a friend. I think the changes only made it stronger.

Q: *What were the biggest challenges in creating book two?*

KAYLA: This one felt more emotional than the previous book in that both girls are dealing with these situations that are extremely personal to them, so putting in scenes where they had to process these difficult emotions was hard—even if I knew things would get better in the end! Tapping into those old feelings of wanting to be accepted and struggling to accept yourself so that you can put that feeling on paper is always a little draining. I cried while planning some of the scenes!

JEFFREY: This book deals with some bigger and weightier issues than ***Work It Out*** did. The challenge we met was finding a way to maintain the high energy and atmosphere of fun that was present in the first book while also working in themes and situations that went into deeper, more serious subjects. So, when writing the script, I thought a lot about how to balance these two aspects of the story and do them both justice. Fortunately, Chanda and Beth are exactly the type of characters to make long, thoughtful conversations about meaningful issues entertaining!

DAMALI: Book two gets to show off a lot of new places like the mall shops, Ms. Foley's house, the surrounding neighborhood, and parks. Bringing all of these unique spaces to life was a challenge, but a fun one!

KRISTINA: This book had some pretty impactful emotional moments for the girls, so capturing the gravity and weight of those scenes was a good challenge! I have so many moments in this book that really resonated with me as a chubbier queer Vietnamese girl in a predominantly white school. I wanted to put in as much love and care while depicting each girl's personal struggles as best as I could. The insecurities we feel aren't always based on something tangible like cruel words or a school bully, it often runs so much deeper than that. And I feel so honored to have had the chance to make a story that really cuts into that topic with Kayla and Jeffrey!

Q: Do you have a favorite scene in the book?

KAYLA: I'm a sucker for dances. I wasn't a big fan of them as a kid, but when it comes to seeing them in graphic novels and movies, I love them. The outfits, the lights, the decorations, the drama—it's such fun!

In terms of the process, Chanda's "Boy Safari" was my favorite to write. I think it might have been the first scene I imagined fully when Jeffrey and I were coming up with the plot.

JEFFREY: I'm partial to the several heart-to-heart conversations that the characters have with one another throughout the book. My favorite is the big talk Chanda and Amaya have that brings their relationship to a better place and sets Chanda on the right path. Sister-sister bonding always hits me right in the feels.

KRISTINA: It's hard to have a favorite! But, if I had to pick, I absolutely love Chanda's "Boy Safari" scene. It's such a hilarious part of the book and so relatable! As someone who really didn't get "liking boys" at all as a teenager, Chanda's whole struggle really resonated with me. Trying to make yourself "have a date" or "be in love" when you just don't feel that way really feels like going through an equation: Me + Boy = Perfect? But life isn't like mathematics. Frankly, it's a lot more complicated and layered, and that's what makes it so interesting and unique to each of us.

DAMALI: I like the scene where Chanda and Beth find out about their classmates' dates. As everyone pairs up, the stakes are raised and the race is on. Olive has two dates! It's really funny.

Q: *In the story, Beth and Chanda struggle to find a way to fit in that also lets them be seen for their individual awesomeness. What do you hope readers will take away from the book?*

KAYLA: I hope readers see Chanda and Beth rocking their uniqueness and feel like they want to do the same in their own lives. Also supporting each other's individuality! Let your friends know what you like about them and why you love them! We all feel self-conscious and down on ourselves sometimes, but hearing something positive from a good friend can really help.

JEFFREY: I think the most important thing kids can do is embrace what makes them unique. There's a lot of pressure—from school, family, friends, society—to check off certain boxes and live up to certain expectations in a particular, predefined way. Chanda and Beth feel that pressure, and it fuels the conflicts in this book. But what if "fitting in" means giving up or trying to change something you love about yourself? The Besties learn to embrace who they are and what they want while tuning out all the feedback around them, and I think that's a mindset to aspire to.

KRISTINA: I had a pretty turbulent relationship with fashion and self-image for most of my youth. It's a misconception that being yourself and loving yourself is easy. It's a struggle for everyone. I really want readers to understand that it is okay to make mistakes, to not always be happy, to have moments of doubt and reflection. And you can rely on other people to be there for you. There is no ultimate form of self-love or self-expression. You'll have bad days that make the world feel like it's falling down. But you'll also have good days that make it all worth it. You're *supposed* to figure yourself out, not just have it all set in stone. So let yourself stumble and breathe the way Beth and Chanda do here. Try new things—don't be afraid to have fun and be weird and be YOU.

DAMALI: I hope readers can learn a little bit about patience through the story. It's really easy if you're feeling self-conscious to either want to fix your problem immediately, or to assume it can't be fixed at all. Chanda and Beth both struggle with this, but a lot of their problems were because they were looking at things the wrong way. By taking time, both girls found solutions that best reflected who they truly are and made them happy. I really think it shows how if we're patient with ourselves and others, things work out for the best.

Q: *Do you have a brief story or something to share about a school dance experience?*

KAYLA: I said earlier that I didn't like dances, which is true of formal dances—mainly because I *hated* shopping for dresses—but I used to love these casual dances in middle school where everyone would hang out in the municipal center's gym. There was a DJ and a snack bar and an air hockey table . . . and no one really worried about dates!

JEFFREY: I have vivid memories of my middle school dances. Only a few kids dressed up, and most spent the majority of the evening huddled around the lunchroom snack tables buying up all the candy and soft drinks that were for sale. (This is where I first learned the joy of drinking Dr Pepper through a sour candy straw.) The dance floor saw a little bit of action, but only when the biggest hits were played. No one could resist the Macarena.

KRISTINA: School dances can and should be fun! But the pressure surrounding them is very real, and I honestly avoided a lot of dances in my youth because of it. I didn't even realize I loved just dancing and how fun it was to go with friends until I was much older. To think I missed out on what could've been a fantastic school-days memory makes me so sad. I think my best dance experiences were ones I went in fully thinking, "I am here to have fun and dance to music I like," and that was it. Tune out the rest of the world and just be there with your friends and have a good time. Nothing else matters. The happiest people at a dance aren't always with a date. The happiest people are always the ones giving 100 percent to the music and just dancing the night away as if no one else is watching. As the book says, find your groove. :)

CREATING THE COVER

Sketches

CREATING THE COVER

Color samples

final cover

DESIGNING THE CHARACTERS

DESIGNING THE CHARACTERS

Line-up of Sam, Beth, Chanda

Line-up of Sam, Beth, Chanda, and all friends

Beth, Chanda, Mr. and Mrs. Basu, Amaya, Seth

A PAGE FROM START TO FINISH

Step 1: panels

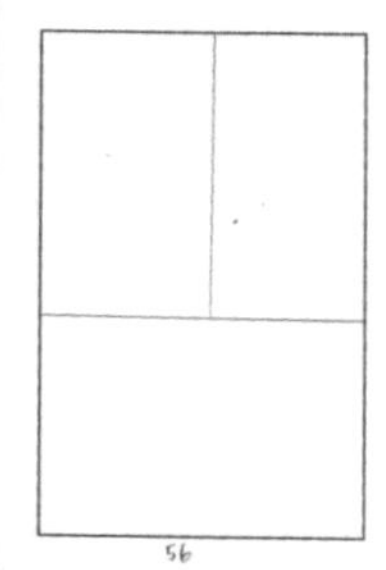

Step 2: thumbnails

Step 3: sketch

Step 4: initial inks

Step 5: final inks

Step 6: final color

ACKNOWLEDGMENTS

First, we'd like to thank Team Besties for bringing another B&C adventure to life! Designer Steph, Letterer Lor, Colorist Damali, and Inking Assistant Victor—this book wouldn't exist without all of your hard work, creativity, and dedication. And a huge thank-you to our amazing, unstoppable collaborator Kristina—it has been a joy and a privilege to work with you on the Besties series. Thank you so much for all of the personality and vibrancy you bring to Chanda, Beth, and their world.

Thank you to everyone at Clarion, especially our editor, Mary—your support in telling these stories in a way that is both sensitive and honest (while still fun and funny!) has meant so much to us.

We'd also like to extend our gratitude to our agent, Elizabeth, for her enthusiasm, wisdom, and encouragement—you rock!

Lastly, the friends and fam: Renée, Mike, Karen, Brad, Grandpa Jeff, William, K, Gabe, Lish, Tyler, Katie, Richard, Erica, Grace—thank you for being our people. Your love and friendship inspires us.

—*Kayla & Jeffrey*

First, I'd like to acknowledge that both Besties books were illustrated on the traditional, ancestral, and unceded territory of many nations, including that of the Coast Salish peoples and the area known as Tkaronto that is home to many diverse First Nations, Inuit, and Métis peoples.

I want to give a huge thank-you to the super-powered folks behind Besties: to Kayla and Jeffrey—for being the best and coolest collaborators I could ever ask for; to Lor—for her fantastic lettering and delightful chats; to Victor—for their amazing background inks and teamwork; to Damali—for her incredible colors that make this book shine; and last but not least, to Britt—for her stalwart support as my agent throughout. It's been such a delight and honor to create the vibrant world of Besties with you all!

And thank you also to my dear friends and family around the world: my C.O.M.I.C. Club friends, Mom, Dad, Bryan, the extended Nguyen family, Molly, and my sweet angel, Milo—may he rest in peace. Your support and love continue to inspire and carry this worm onward.

And lastly, thank you, dear reader, for picking up this book! I hope it brings you joy as it has for me.

—*Kristina*

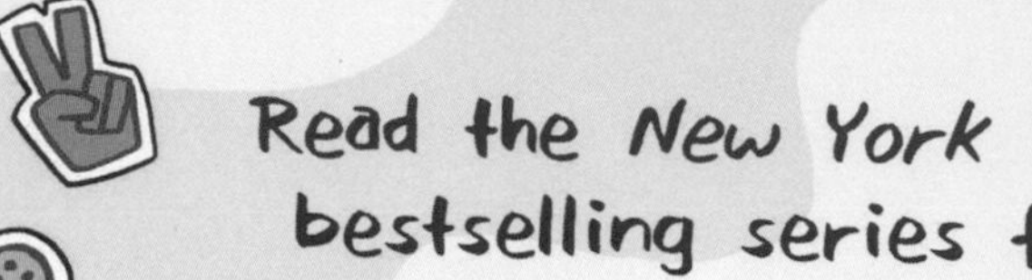

Read the *New York Times* bestselling series from Kayla Miller

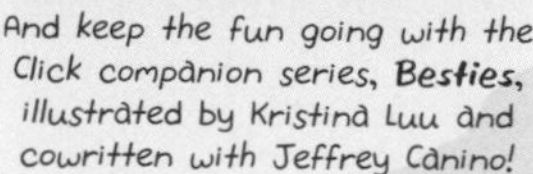

And keep the fun going with the Click companion series, **Besties**, illustrated by Kristina Luu and cowritten with Jeffrey Canino!